In memory of Mum and Dad
who took us to the beach.

First published 1996
A Little Ark Book
Allen & Unwin Pty Ltd
9 Atchison Street
St Leonards, NSW 2065
Australia

Phone: (61 2) 9901 4088
Fax: (61 2) 9906 2218
E-mail: 100252.103@compuserve.com

1 3 5 7 9 10 8 6 4 2

National Library of Australia
Cataloguing-in-Publication entry:

Honey, Elizabeth, 1947- .
Not a nibble!

ISBN 1 86448 099 8.
ISBN 1 86448 242 7 (pbk.).

I. Title.

A823.3

Designed by Elizabeth Honey and Tou-Can Design
Printed in Hong Kong by Dah Hua Printing

Not a Nibble!

Elizabeth Honey

A LITTLE ARK BOOK

ALLEN & UNWIN

'Goodbye smelly old city!' yelled Alex.
'Hello big blue sea!' sang Susie.
Tucki sat on his goggles,
cousin Vin counted his pocket-money
and Mum asked Dad if he'd locked the back door.

'A spot of fishing,' said Dad. 'That's what I need!'

'I need a swim!' said Tucki.

'I'm going to catch a fish,' said Susie.

The first day.

Dad whistled as he made a cup of tea.

'Wake up, you limpets! Who's coming fishing?'

'Me! Me! Me!' said the kids.

''Bye,' said Mum with a lazy smile. 'Good luck!'

It was cold as they walked to the rocks.

The sky was like pale blue glass.

Vin pounced. 'I found a cowrie!'

'Hey, there's crabs in this pool!' yelled Tucki.

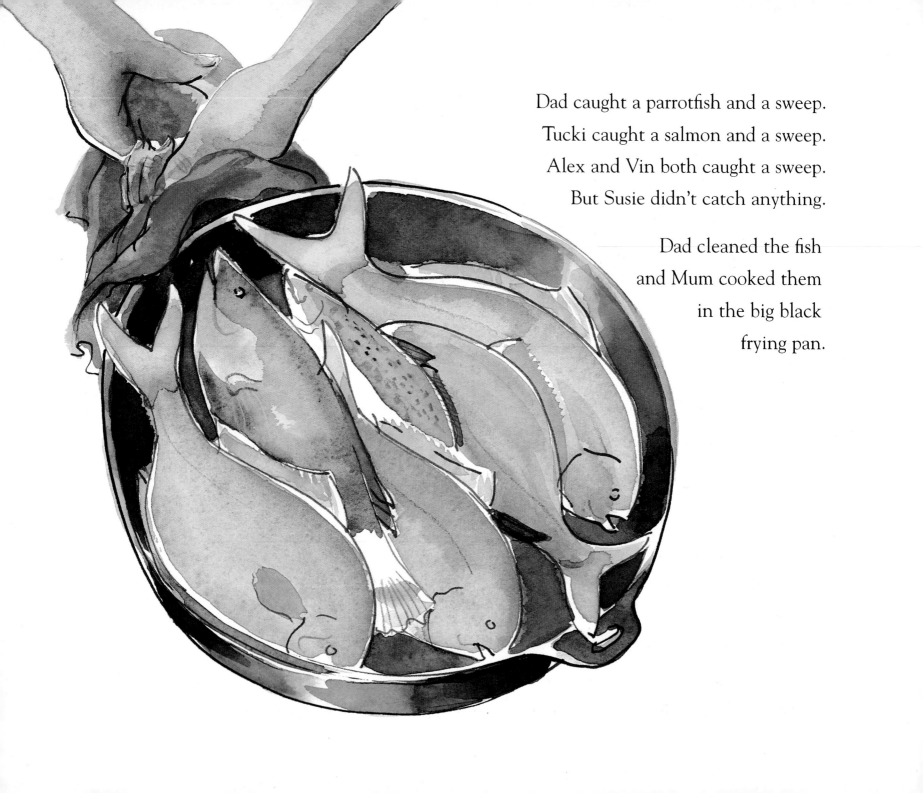

Dad caught a parrotfish and a sweep.
Tucki caught a salmon and a sweep.
Alex and Vin both caught a sweep.
But Susie didn't catch anything.

Dad cleaned the fish
and Mum cooked them
in the big black
frying pan.

The second day.

A slash of sun in the tent flap.

'Wake up, you stunned mullets!' said Dad. 'Who's coming fishing?'

'Me,' said Vin.

Alex yawned. 'I'm going to play with the kids next door.'

Tucki mumbled, 'Don't wake me now, Dad, I'm in the middle of a good dream…'

'Well, *I* know what *I'm* going to do,' said Susie. '*I'm* going to catch a fish!'

They fished from the old swing bridge.
Vin and Susie threw sticks into the river
and watched them slowly drift to the sea.
They felt warm and drowsy.
Vin caught a tiddler and threw it back.

For lunch they bought pies and chips.
They were sunburnt behind the knees.

'Did you catch a fish, love?'
 asked the lady in the caravan
 next door.
'Not yet,' said Susie.

The third day.

'Wake up, you lobsters!' said Dad.

'It's a bit chilly this morning.
Who's coming fishing?'

'Me,' said Tucki and Vin.

'Not me,' said Alex.

'Me,' said Susie.

'I'm going to catch a fish.'

'You put on jackets
and caps,' said Mum,
'or you'll catch
a cold as well.'

On the pier it was freezing.

They sat in the lee of a boat, out of the wind.

They teased the seagulls and tried to feed the one with the missing leg.

The fish were biting. Dad caught a couta and a squid.

Tucki caught two salmon and a leatherjacket.

Vin caught a King George whiting.

But Susie didn't catch anything.

'How did the fishing go, Susie?'
asked Mrs Butler in the milk bar.
'Not good,' said Susie.
'I haven't caught a fish yet.'

The fourth day.
It was raining.
Everybody stayed snug in bed.

They read comics, got up late,
had sausages and bacon and eggs,
and played mad Monopoly
all afternoon.
Moneybags Mum had six hotels.

The fifth day.
A clear blue sky.
'Wake up, you flatheads!' said Dad.
'Let's try our luck off the bottom
of the pier. Who's coming fishing?'
'No thanks,' said Vin and Alex.
'OK,' said Tucki.
'Me,' said Susie.
'I'm going to catch a fish.'

'Susie! *Quick!*' yelled Dad.

'You've got a bite!'

Something was tugging hard.

Susie reeled in fast.

Suddenly the line bounced free.

Her hook and sinker were gone.

'Bad luck!' said Dad. 'You nearly had it.'

Dad caught two salmon,
Tucki caught three,
and Susie said, '*Stupid stupid fishing!*'

'Any luck, Susie?'
asked Mr Blonski, the newsagent.
'No luck,' sighed Susie.

Second last day.
'Great morning, shark bait,' said Dad.
'Who's coming fishing?'
'Not me,' said Tucki.
'No thanks,' said Vin.
'OK,' said Alex.
'Would you like to come to the market with
me, Susie?' asked Mum. 'We can have lunch in
the cafe with those big frothy milk shakes.'
'No,' said Susie. 'I'm going to catch a fish.'

They tried their luck from the bridge again.

Dad caught two bream.

Alex caught a mullet.

'Hey, Susie! There's something
on your line,' yelled Alex.
Quickly Susie reeled in, but it was
only a fish cut out of seaweed.
'*Alex!*' growled Dad.
'It's not funny,' said Susie.

'Were they biting today, Susie?'
asked Mr Avanetti, the baker.
'Not for me, they weren't,' said Susie.

The last day.
'Well, you sea urchins,' said Dad.
Who's coming fishing?'
Silence.
Everybody looked at Susie.
She smiled.
'Me,' said Susie, cheerfully.
'Today I'm really going to catch a fish.'
'Good luck, little fishergirl,' said Mum.
'You know, some people never catch a fish.
They're just not lucky at catching fish.'

The water was clear and sparkling.
Susie sat still.
'Be *quiet!*' she told the seagulls.
'I'm trying to catch a fish.'

The morning drifted on.
Not a nibble.

'It's nearly lunchtime,
sweetheart, we'll have to
head back,' said Dad.
It was the last day.
Susie hadn't caught a fish.

Susie blinked back the tears.

In the whole wide sea there was nothing for her.

She stared at the water.

Then, in the smooth silver waves
a dark shape caught her eye.

'Dad, look!' gasped Susie. 'I think it's…a whale…'
But the shape disappeared.

'A whale? Where? I can't see anything.
Come on, Susie,' said Dad.
'Let's head back.'

Susie glared at the sea.
Stupid tricking sea.

'Wouldn't be a whale,'
said an old fisherman.
'Haven't seen a whale
here for years.'

Then two huge shapes slowly surfaced.

'It *is* a whale…and it's got *a baby!*' yelled Susie.

'By jove, you're right!' said the fisherman.
 Everybody raced to the end of the pier.
'They'd be southern right whales.'
'A baby whale is called a calf.'
'They breathe air, you know, but they can stay
 underwater for half an hour!'
'They eat krill. Is there krill in this water?'
'They sing to each other.
 Wonder if they're singing to each other now?'

Everybody knew something
amazing about whales.

Then the mother whale rose out of the water,
almost as if she was showing them
her magnificent crusty head.
They could see her eye and her long,
curved, upside-down mouth.
Mother whale fell back with a walloping splash.

A slow graceful flip of their tails,
and the whales were gone.

'She *smiled* at me!' laughed Susie.

Dad and Susie hurried back.
At the milk bar, the newsagent's and
the baker's, Susie flew in to tell her news.

Susie dashed through the camping park.

She flung open the tent flap.

'Guess what!'

'You caught a fish?'

'Better than a fish.

Anyone can catch a fish!' said Susie,

hopping from one foot to the other.

'Bigger than sixty fish!

Bigger than our *house!*'

'Pull the other leg,' said Tucki.

'No,' said Dad. 'It's true!'

'I spotted *two whales!*' said Susie.

'A mother and a calf!'

'I'm not lucky at fishing,' said Susie,

'but *I'm* the lucky one at spotting whales!'